Hi, I'm **Carrie**

And I'm **David**

Welcome to our **JUMP UP** and **JOIN IN** series.

We hope you enjoy reading the books and joining in with the songs.

This book is called **Giraffe's Big Night**.

All the animals work together and it helps us to learn about **singing safely**.

That's great. Remember to **turn the page** when you hear this sound . . .

oooooo!

EGMONT
We bring stories to life

First published in Great Britain 2014
by Egmont UK Limited,
The Yellow Building, 1 Nicholas Road, London W11 4AN
www.egmont.co.uk

Text copyright © Carrie and David Grant 2014
Illustrations copyright © Ailie Busby 2014

Carrie and David Grant and Ailie Busby have asserted their moral rights.

ISBN 978 1 4052 5837 1

A CIP catalogue record for this title is available from the British Library.

For our gorgeous
children who are
learning the importance
of friendship.
– Carrie and David –

For Mum (never
too busy to listen).
– Ailie –

Carrie and David Grant

Giraffe's Big Night

Illustrations by Ailie Busby

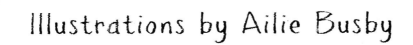

Remember to turn the page when Giraffe goes ooOOO!

EGMONT

Giraffe had been chosen
to sing at the opera because
she had such a strong voice.

La la la la LA LA LA!

It was her **big** chance to fulfil her dream of becoming a singer.

All week, Giraffe practised singing
very hard and very loudly.
A little TOO loudly!

Giraffe woke up with a sore throat.

"I'll never make it to the o-o-o-opera," she whimpered. "I'm as hoarse as a horse!"

Giraffe's friends were **very** worried. There were only a few days to go and Giraffe's voice sounded like a little mouse squeaking.

The doctor came to visit.
"You need to drink plenty of water,
stay quiet and keep warm," he advised.

Elephant brought Giraffe
lots of water.

Meerkat made sure Giraffe stayed very quiet.

Monkey kept Giraffe's
throat cosy and warm.

Soon Giraffe started to feel better.
"Do-Re-Mi . . ." she sang,

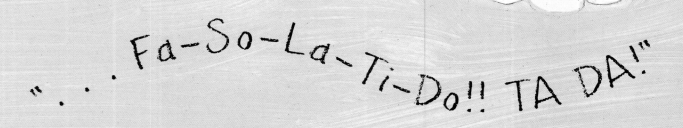

". . . Fa-So-La-Ti-Do!! TA DA!"

Now Giraffe was
really ready!

That night all Giraffe's friends
went to the opera to watch her.

They were very nervous — would Giraffe's strong voice make a miraculous recovery?

Giraffe gave an amazing performance!

"Thank you, my friends!" she cried. "You really helped make my dream come true!"

Gotta Be Ready *sing-along song*

Chorus:
I gotta be ready,
Gotta be ready,
Gotta be ready,
For tonight!

I got my friends,
I can rely,
I gotta get ready for tonight!
I got my sisters,
Got my brothers,
They surround me
Like no others!
Got my supporters,
Got my fans,
They want to give me a helping hand.
It's curtain up, light the lights,
I gotta be ready for tonight!

Chorus:
I gotta be ready,
Gotta be ready,
Gotta be ready,
For tonight!
I gotta be ready,
Gotta be ready,

Gotta be ready,
For tonight!

Friends call and text me,
Send me a letter,
They are hoping that I'll be better.
Cos it's showtime for my singing,
It's my future and my beginning!
I need my soul, need my stride,
I need my voice and my style.
For curtain up, light the lights,
I gotta be ready for tonight!

Chorus:
I gotta be ready,
Gotta be ready,
Gotta be ready,
For tonight!
I gotta be ready,
Gotta be ready,
Gotta be ready,
For tonight!

And then they call me,
Giraffe, you're the best
    singer that I know!

I think you're fantastic,
I can't wait to see you tonight,
It's gonna be amazing!

And then they call me,
Hi, sis, have a great show tonight,
Keep the faith,
Keep the good voice,
I'm really watching out for you!

And then they call me,
Giraffe, we're your biggest fans,
You know we love you.
We're gonna be there on the
   front row tonight,
Waving and cheering. Be great!

And then they call me,
This is your singing teacher,
   remember to warm up!

Chorus:
I gotta be ready,
Gotta be ready,
Gotta be ready,
For tonight!
I gotta be ready,
Gotta be ready,
Gotta be ready,
For tonight!
I gotta be ready,
Gotta be ready,
Gotta be ready,
For tonight!
I gotta be ready,
Gotta be ready,
Gotta be ready,
For tonight!

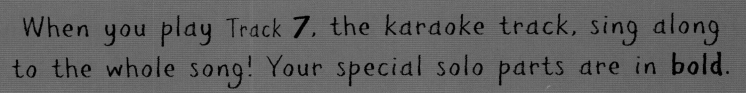

When you play Track **7**, the karaoke track, sing along
to the whole song! Your special solo parts are in **bold**.

Singing Safely!

We hope you enjoyed the story.
This story was all about singing safely.

We don't want to whisper when we sing,
but we don't want to shout either.
Somewhere in the middle is good.

You should always breathe **deeply**, keep your shoulders down – and keep your chin down too.

Breathe in and sing from one to five with your middle volume.

Not too **loud** . . .

. . . and not too quiet.

Like this . . .

One, two, three, four, five.

For our **Jump Up** and **Join In** series we really want to get children interested in music and how it works. It shouldn't be rocket science and we want to encourage you as a parent, teacher or carer to teach your children with confidence. If **you** can learn it then **you** can pass it on.

Track 6 ## Singing Sirens!

So in this book we're going to move on to singing High and Low.

First let's try to speak really **low** and **slow**, just like this:

Jump up and join in!

Now let's try to speak really high and fast, like this:

Jump up and join in!

Now let's add more of a note to that. Try to be a police car siren, like this:

WHAH-OH-WHAH-OH

Now let's try to add a **low** note to our sound. We're going to yawn like a big old bear:

YAWN

Make your own
Blow Bottles!

You'll need: Plastic bottles of all different shapes and sizes (up to ten types)

Water   Food colouring   Funnel   Plastic jug

Ask a grown-up to help you!

Step 1 Line up your bottles – it doesn't matter in what order.

Step 2 Use the funnel and jug to fill the bottles with different levels of water.

Step 3 Drop different coloured food colouring into each bottle. This is just to make them look pretty!

Step 4 Blow across the top of each bottle in any order. They will all make different sounds!

Now look after your voice just like Giraffe – you can still make a sound by blowing softly!

About Carrie and David

Carrie and David are best known for their hugely successful CBeebies series, **Carrie and David's Popshop**. They have coached Take That, The Saturdays and the Spice Girls and have a top-selling vocal coaching book and DVD. In 2008 they were awarded a BASCA for their lifetime services to the music industry.

Parents to four children, Carrie and David are passionate about getting all children to sing and are keen to encourage adults to feel more confident in teaching their little ones music skills from an early age. The **Jump Up And Join In** series was born as a result of this passion and will help young children learn a set of basic skills and develop a real love of music. As ambassadors for **Sing Up** – a not-for-profit organisation providing the complete singing solution for schools – and judges of the young singers on BBC 1's **Comic Relief Does Glee Club**, Carrie and David believe children everywhere should be given the tools to enjoy, and to feel confident about, practising music in all its shapes and forms.

Thanks for jumping up
and joining in!
Till the next time, bye!